Angela's Airplane

Story • Robert Munsch
Art • Michael Martchenko

Annick Press Ltd.   Toronto, Canada

Fifth Printing, June, 1990

Annick Press gratefully acknowledges the contributions of the Canada Council and The Ontario Arts Council

Canadian Cataloguing in Publication Data

Munsch, Robert N., 1945-
Angela's airplane

(Munsch for kids)
ISBN 1-55037-027-8 (bound). — ISBN 1-55037-026-X (pbk.)

I. Martchenko, Michael. II. Title. III. Series:
Munsch, Robert N., 1945-   . Munsch for kids.

PS8576.U58A82 1988   C813'.54   C88-094111-1
PZ7.M86An 1988

Distributed in Canada and the U.S.A. by:
Firefly Books Ltd.
250 Sparks Avenue
Willowdale, Ontario
M2H 2S4 Canada

 Printed on acid free paper

Printed and bound in Canada by
D.W. Friesen & Sons

To Candy Christianson

Angela's father took her to the airport, but when they got there, a terrible thing happened. Angela's father got lost.

Angela looked under airplanes and on top of airplanes and beside airplanes but she couldn't find him any place, so Angela decided to look inside an airplane.

She saw one with an open door and climbed up the steps: One, two, three, four, five, six; right to the top. Her father was not there, and neither was anyone else.

Angela had never been in an airplane before. In the front there was a seat that had lots of buttons all around it. Angela loved to push buttons, so she walked up to the front, sat down in the seat and said to herself, "It's okay if I push just *one* button. Don't you think it's okay if I push just *one* button? Oh yes, it's okay. Yes, yes, yes, yes." Then she slowly pressed the bright red button. Right away the door closed.

Angela said, "It's okay if I push just one more button. Don't you think it's okay if I push just one more button? Oh yes, it's okay. Yes, yes, yes, yes." Slowly, she pushed the yellow button. Right away the lights came on.

Angela said, "It's okay if I push just *one more* button. Don't you think it's okay if I push just *one more* button? Oh yes, it's okay. Yes, yes, yes, yes." She pushed the green button. Right away the motor came on, VROOM, VROOM, VROOM, VROOM.

Angela said, "Yikes," and pushed all the buttons at once. The airplane took off and went right up into the air.

When Angela looked out the window she saw that she was very high in the sky. She didn't know how to get down. The only thing to do was to push one more button, so she slowly pushed the black button. It was the radio button. A voice came on the radio and said, "Bring back that airplane, you thief, you."

Angela said, "My name is Angela. I am five years old and I don't know how to fly airplanes."

"Oh dear," said the voice. "What a mess. Listen very carefully, Angela. Take the steering wheel and turn it to the left."

Angela turned the wheel and very slowly the airplane went in a big circle and came back right over the airport.

"Okay," said the voice, "now pull back on the wheel."

Angela pulled back on the wheel and the airplane slowly went down to the runway. It hit once and bounced. It hit again and bounced. Then one wing scraped the ground. Right away the whole plane smashed and broke into little pieces.

Angela was left sitting on the ground and she didn't even have a scratch.

All sorts of cars and trucks came speeding out of the terminal.

There were police cars, ambulances, fire trucks and buses. And all sorts of people came running, but in front of everybody was Angela's father.

He picked her up and said, "Angela, are you all right?"

"Yes," said Angela.

"Oh, Angela," he said, "the airplane is not all right. It is in very small pieces."

"I know," said Angela, "It was a mistake."

"Well, Angela," said her father, "promise me you will never fly another airplane."

"I promise," said Angela.

"Are you sure?" said the father.

Angela said very loudly, "I promise, I promise, I promise."

Angela didn't fly an airplane for a very long time. But when she grew up she didn't become a doctor, she didn't become a truck driver, she didn't become a secretary and she didn't become a nurse. She became an airplane pilot.